Karim Pieritz

Lighthouse of Adventure

for Beginning Readers 1

The Magical Dinosaur Hunting

 1

This book belongs to: _____

Started reading on: _____

Finished reading on: _____

2

Inhalt

Hello, my name is Billy!

 4

Long ago, I was enchanted. Since then I have been a storybook.

I know a lot of great stories about dinosaurs, pirates and wizards.

Believe it or not, I have been in all these adventures!

Today I want to tell you about Michael.

Michael does not know it yet, but he is going on a journey.

A journey to another planet!

This is Michael.

Evergreen

Michael is 8 years old. He lives in a city with a beautiful forest. There is an oak tree that never loses its leaves. The inhabitants of the village called it "Magical Oak". They even named their city Evergreen.

Michael is in the forest. He is looking for a stick to use as a sword.

Suddenly, a small creature appears in a knothole. It is a boy named Nathaniel.

This is Nathaniel.

 8

Nathaniel is 9 years old. He gives Michael a colorful flashlight.

When he disappears in the knothole, he loses his storybook. It is a talking book. Which talking book do you think it is? It's me, of course!

Fortunately Michael finds me and takes me with him. Who knows what would otherwise have happened to me?

The flashlight

Michael is back at home again and I tell him about the flashlight. If you look into the light, you will fly to the planet Blue Sky.

Then I show him a map of Blue Sky.

The sea is blue. The country is yellow and green. A volcano spits out red hot lava.

There are elves, dwarves, pirates, giants and many other magical creatures.

On one side of the planet the sun always shines. On the other side it is always dark.

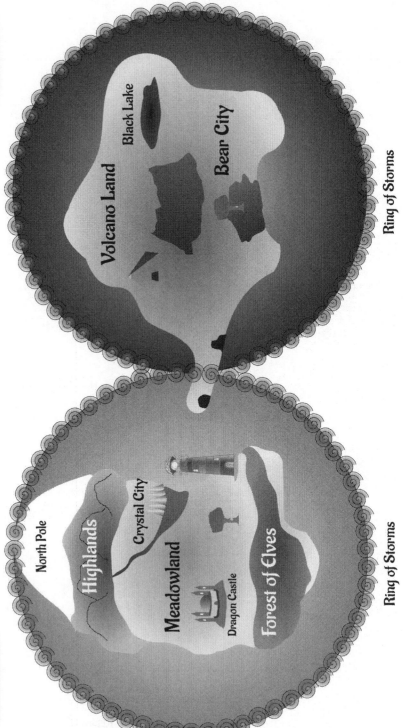

Blue Sky

Bright side

Dark side

North Pole

Highlands

Crystal City

Meadowland

Dragon Castle

Forest of Elves

Volcano Land

Black Lake

Bear City

Ring of Storms

Ring of Storms

The lighthouse

Michael takes the lamp and looks into the light. He travels through space and, as promised, lands on Blue Sky.

He stands on a meadow near a brightly painted lighthouse. It is the "Lighthouse of Adventure".

Michael looks at the colors: red, orange, yellow, green, blue, indigo, violet. It is a rainbow!

Nathaniel runs out of the lighthouse towards Michael.

 14

Nathaniel is excited by Michael's visit. He takes him to the lighthouse. Although it is strictly forbidden, he leads Michael up to the lamp. The lamp is a crystal. It is the source of magic on Blue Sky.

Nathaniel throws an apple into the crystal and it just flies through. Michael catches the apple and is amazed. It has turned into a tomato!

Michael throws back the tomato and Nathaniel catches it. It has turned into a coconut!

Suddenly they hear a loud crash. Michael looks out of the window and cannot believe his eyes. A Tyrannosaurus Rex is destroying a small shed!

Nathaniel explains that the dinosaur does not belong to Blue Sky. He has to be sent back to earth. For this they have to use the magical flashlight. Nathaniel gives him a blue lamp and they go outside.

The butterfly

Nathaniel and Michael are standing in the meadow in front of the lighthouse. Nathaniel blows a small whistle. Michael cannot hear anything, but suddenly the sun darkens. A giant butterfly lands right in front of them. A strong wind sweeps Michael off his feet.

Michael does not know what is happening to him. Suddenly he is sitting behind Nathaniel in the saddle and they fly to the sky.

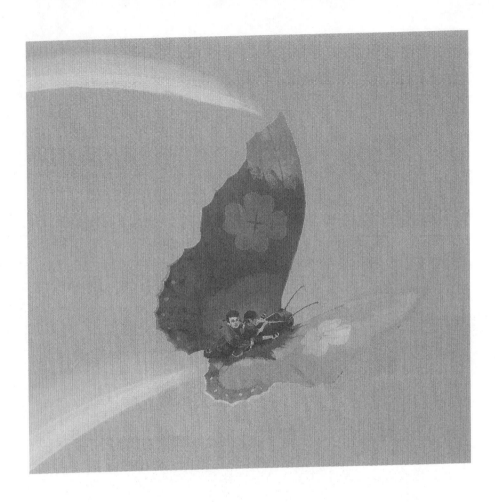

The world below him becomes tiny. Nathaniel shows him the Dragon Castle, where his father is working as a wizard. Nathaniel also wants to be a wizard, someday.

 18

The hunt

Nathaniel flies with his butterfly towards the dangerous dinosaur. Michael aims the flashlight at him, but what happens? The T.Rex jumps and tries to catch them!

They fly higher and higher, and now they are being hunted. Again and again the dinosaur jumps high into the air. The butterfly stumbles. Michael falls off the saddle and plunges into the depths! The open mouth of the dinosaur is waiting for him.

 20

Michael believes that his end is near. But Nathaniel pulls the butterfly into an incredible looping and catches him in the last second.

Again Michael sits firmly in the saddle and Nathaniel goes into a nosedive. Michael aims his flashlight at the dinosaur. Again he jumps up at them! But this time Michael is faster.

He switches on the lamp and the dinosaur disappears with a bang.

Nathaniel lands the butterfly and they descend. Michael's knees are quite weak. He will never forget this adventure. He gives Nathaniel the flashlight and then he looks into the light.

Again he flies through the universe and lands in his bed. With a pounding heart and a smile on his face, he falls asleep.

The Dinopark

The next day Michael's class visits a dinosaur park. Michael and his friend Tim decide to race. Who will be the first at the T.Rex? The figure looks like the dinosaur from Blue Sky. How is that possible? Suddenly the dinosaur opens his mouth!

 23

But fortunately, the dinosaur just yawns. He talks and introduces himself as Rexi. He does not know why he is alive. He is sorry about chasing the butterfly. He likes the Dinopark and wants to stay there. In the moonlight he goes hunting. Michael hopes that he would not hunt people.

The Laser Gun

During the afternoon back at school there is a quarrel. The new classmate Jack has kicked a football at Tim's head.

This is Jack.

Tim's face reddens and he goes to Jack. Jack tells him about his mighty "laser gun". He has burst the dinosaur-balloons in the park and he threatens to do this Tim.

Now Michael knows that Jack has a magical flashlight too! He tries to explain the lamp, but Jack does not believe him and goes home.

Michael is worried, but Nathaniel will know what to do. The weekend has begun and Michael is looking forward to his more trips to Blue Sky.

The End

Questions

1. Evergreen is called that, because there is a magical ...
2. Michael gets the magical flashlight from ...
3. With a magical flashlight you can travel to ...
4. The lighthouse is painted like a ...
5. Nathaniel uses his whistle to call a ...

Answers

5. Butterfly
4. Rainbow
3. Planet Blue Sky
2. Nathaniel
1. Oak tree

28

Coloring Page

 29

Verlag Karim Pieritz
Kinderbücher und mehr!

Books from Karim Pieritz:

- ISBN 978-1503085060 (German): Die magische Dinosaurier-Jagd
- **ISBN 978-1515001676 (English): The Magical Dinosaur Hunt**
- ISBN 978-3944626314 (English-German bilingual):
  Die magische Dinosaurier-Jagd - The Magical Dinosaur Hunt

www.karimpieritz.de

Illustrations: Markus Lenz
Map: Karim Pieritz
Headlines: Google Web Font Aladin

The story is fictional.
Any resemblance to real names or events is purely coincidental.

Made in the USA
Lexington, KY
02 July 2018